Jonathan Smyth

Cowboy Sleuth

BOOK FIVE

The Case of the Deathly Water Babies of Pyramid Lake

Frank F. Fiore

Jonathan Smyth
Cowboy Sleuth

BOOK FIVE

The Case of the Deathly
Water Babies of Pyramid Lake

Frank F. Fiore

STORY BACKGROUND

THE SMYTH NOVELS ARE A NEW TWIST ON THE STANDARD WESTERN. THEY PIT THE BEST OF THE BRITISH AGAINST THE AMERICAN WEST, FILLED with action, drama, twists, turns, and gunfights.

Jack the Ripper is terrorizing the citizens of London, and there is only one connection between each murder known to the police - an amateur sleuth called Jonathan Smyth. After a particularly grizzly murder, the fickle finger of fate points directly at Smyth, who cannot be located. When Scotland Yard discovers that their prime suspect has seemingly fled to the fledgling United States, they send one of their best men, Charles Abbott, after him.

Smyth, an intrepid sleuth, is caught in a new land filled with legends, mysteries and horrors. His goal is to unmask the Ripper when he commits his gruesome and horrible murders again in the Wild West.

PROLOGUE

The icy wind whipped across Pyramid Lake, etching goosebumps onto Pahninee's sunbaked skin. His weathered hands gripped the oars, propelling his small fishing boat through the pewter-gray water. The silence was only broken by the rhythmic creak of the oars and the mournful cry of a distant loon.

For decades, Pahninee had fished for the Cui-ui, which is only found in these waters. His boat a second skin, the lake his familiar, if unforgiving, mistress. Yet, a gnawing unease gnawed at his gut today. Whispers had drifted ashore - whispers of a missing fisherman. His old friend, Tau-gu, vanished without a trace a week ago.

But Tau-gu's disappearance wasn't the first.

Several others had gone missing over the past months, swallowed up by the lake's murky depths without a ripple of explanation.

The legend of the Pyramid Lake Water Babies, whispered in dusty saloons and around crackling campfires, felt real for the first time. A phantom stalker haunting the Nevada desert, leaving a trail of blood in its wake.

He scanned the water, eyes searching for any unnatural movement. The wind seemed to mock him, whipping the waves into frenzied whitecaps.

Suddenly, a flicker of movement caught his eye. A flash of red, like a poppy blooming against the gray water. He squinted, heart hammering against his ribs. A skiff, bobbing erratically near the distant shore, its sail hanging slack like a shroud.

Fear battled curiosity, but the fisherman in Pahninee refused to ignore a possible distress call. He dug his oars deeper into the water, the boat slicing through the choppy waves like a determined blade. As he drew closer, a sense of dread hung heavy in the air. The red flash resolved into a man's jacket, half-submerged in the water, staining the lake with a vivid, morbid hue.

Pahninee's stomach lurched. He knew, with icy certainty, what he would find. He slowed the boat - his movements numb with dread. Reaching for the jacket, he pulled it free, revealing a pale face beneath, eyes open wide in eternal surprise. A thin red line, almost too neat to be real, marred the throat.

Tau-gu!

His face held a silent scream, a frozen echo of the horror. Pahninee fell back against the boat, nausea rising in his throat, fear replacing curiosity like a cold hand gripping his heart.

THE CASE OF THE DEATHLY WATER BABIES OF PYRAMID LAKE

The Pyramid Lake Deathly Water Babies weren't a whisper anymore. It was a reality, a monster breathing the same thin air, casting its bloody shadow across the water. And Pahninee's, alone on his boat, had just come face to face with it.

The wind seemed to howl across the lake, hearing the dejected cries of an invisible baby and the laughter of ghostly children. He knew such sounds carried with them a warning according to the Pyramid Lake natives. As the Paiute tell it, "If you hear it, it's bad news; if you see it, you're dead!"

As darkness embraced the lake, only one question remained, chilling and unanswered: who would be next?

CHAPTER ONE

The Nevada sun beat down like a blacksmith's hammer on Reno as Smyth and Abbott disembarked the Central Pacific train. Sweat beaded on Abbott's brow, a stark contrast to Smyth's stoic composure.

"How do you manage to stay so composed in this inferno?" Abbott mused, dabbing at his brow. "The heat's practically suffocating."

"Years in Her Majesty's Calvary in the Sudan will do that to a man," Smyth quipped with a nonchalant shrug. "You acclimate." The amateur British sleuth surveyed their surroundings. "Now, let's locate this hotel and inquire about those mysterious murders at Pyramid Lake."

"Do we even have a hotel in mind?" Abbott inquired.

"The Riverside," Smyth answered confidently. "Supposed to be top-notch for this town, according to Inspector Hardon back in Prescott. Said we'd find it rather cushy."

With determined strides, the duo made their way towards the Truckee River and the Riverside Hotel, a wooden building erected in 1868, proudly standing next to the first bridge that dared to span the tempestuous Truckee River in the mid-1800s.

"Not too shabby," Abbott remarked, eyeing the establishment. "Looks like we'll finally get to rest our weary bones in a proper bed."

Stepping into the three-story edifice, adorned with rows of windows that seemed to stretch forever, Smyth and Abbott were greeted by the sight of an affable clerk, clad in a snazzy blue paisley suit and sporting a meticulously groomed beard.

"Welcome, to the Riverside, gentlemen," the clerk greeted with an amiable smile. "How may I be of service?"

"We require lodgings for two," Smyth stated plainly.

"Certainly. And the names for the register?"

"Jonathan Smyth and Charles Abbott."

"Smyth and Abbott?" the clerk's eyes twinkled in recognition. "Ah, yes. You're already registered in one of our finest suites."

"Already registered?" Smyth raised an eyebrow in confusion. "By whom?"

Before the clerk could stammer a reply, a voice, sharp as a Highland wind, sliced through the air. "Hello, Jonathan. Took your time getting here."

A fiery redhead materialized behind them, a whirlwind of contradictions. Petite but fierce, doe-eyed yet steely. She sported a white blouse that strained against a bosom accentuated by a black, split-leg jumpsuit that wouldn't look out of place on a Cossack dancer. Topped it all off with a ridiculous Aussie hat perched precariously on her flaming locks.

"No worries," she continued, not waiting for a response. "Your delay gave me time to poke around. And find Wovoka."

Smyth, speechless for a moment, was struck not just by her beauty but by her sheer audacity. "Who are you?" he finally managed - his voice tight. "And what gives you the right to use my first name?"

A perfectly manicured hand landed on her hip. "Now, now," she drawled, the hint of a Scottish brogue lacing her words. "Fellow investigators, aren't we? And like your chum Charles here, journalists too."

Smyth regained some composure and scoffed. "That doesn't explain who you are or why you're here."

The redhead's smile turned razor sharp. "The name's Bessie McDonald. Bessie with a B, darling. Reporter for the Chicago Democrat. But you can call me Bess."

"A reporter?" Abbott echoed, eyebrows raised.

Bess threw her head back and laughed, a sound that could curdle milk. "Is that so surprising? I do have a degree in Journalism, you know. From the esteemed University of Missouri. Graduated Summa Cum Laude, no less."

"The surprising part," Abbott cut in, a smirk playing on his lips, "is that you're actually employed as a reporter. Did you, perhaps," eyeing her curvature frame, "use some, uh... unconventional methods to secure that position?" His voice hardened. "Or are you one of those pesky suffragettes causing all the ruckus?"

Bess's eyes narrowed. "Well, yes and no," she said, her voice clipped. "Let's just say my father..." she drew closer to Abbott, "owns the newspaper?"

Smyth snorted. "American nepotism."

Bess's smile vanished completely. "Don't underestimate me, Mr. Smyth." Her voice accentuated his name. "I may look like a firecracker, but I'm a damn good reporter. Cracked several high-profile murder cases in Chicago. Interested in the details?"

Smyth, clearly flustered, shook his head. "Not particularly. What I do care about is *why* you're here and *how* you found us."

Bess leaned in, a conspiratorial glint in her eyes. "Word travels fast. Your little escapade in Prescott, and now this Jack the Ripper business? All the rage on the wires, thanks to a helpful Wells Fargo inspector in Prescott who filled me in on your destination." She winked. "So, here I am."

"You mentioned someone named Wovoka," Abbott interjected, sensing a shift in the conversation.

Bess's eyes brightened. "Yes. But maybe we should sit down and bring you up to date on what I found. Better than standing here in the lobby."

"Why would we be interested in what you found?" Smyth remarked.

"Would Confederate gold interest you, luv?"

Abbott's eyes turned to Smyth. "Do you think...?"

Smyth brought his finger to his lips to hush Abbott. "What do you know about Confederate gold?"

"Only that it was involved with your Prescott affair," she replied.

"That has nothing to do with why we are here, Smyth stated. "We're investigating the brutal killings on the lake."

"Ah yes," Bess replied. "You think it's the Ripper, huh?" With a twinkle in her eyes, she replied, "Then you need to talk to Wovoka."

"A lead is a lead," Abbott conceded.

Smyth nodded.

She turned to the clerk. "Is there some place we can talk in private?"

The clerk, still slightly flustered by the fiery redhead, quickly pointed to a doorway on the right. "Certainly, ma'am. Right this way."

After following the clerk to a small anteroom, the trio settled into plush armchairs around a low cocktail table. Bess, ever the picture of confidence, crossed her legs and took a deep breath. "What do you know of the lake?"

"Only reports of the murders there," Smyth replied.

"Well, here's what I found out." Bess sat back leisurely in her chair and began.

"Pyramid Lake get its name from the irregular rocky pyramid formations jutting above the waterline. It's located within the Pyramid Lake Paiute Tribe Reservation and quite large for the desert here. Over 15 miles long and11 mile wide with depths reaching over 350 feet."

"Those stones jotting out of the lake are very majestic," she added. "But those stones are nothing compared to what lies beneath the water." She paused. "I'm parched. Could we order something to drink?"

Abbott volunteered. "What would the lady like?"

"Mmm...Champagne, of course."

"Just get us a couple of beers, Abbott," Smyth clipped.

Abbott wandered off while Smyth asked, "So what does this geology discussion have to do with the Ripper?"

"You should know the legend of the lake. The legend of the water babies that surrounds the lake." She straightened up as to lecture. "It goes like this. Mysterious and dangerous spirits are said to mimic the sounds of crying babies to lure in victims."

Abbott returned just then with the beers and Bess's champagne when he overheard Bess's mention of spirits. A distressed Abbott piped up. "Oh, God. It had to be spirits."

Bess ignored Abbott's verbal hand wringing.

She continued. "There are many legends surrounding the origin of the water babies. One version holds that premature or malformed infants were thrown into the waters to maintain the strength of the tribe. According to another version, a Paiute tribesman fell in love with a mermaid from the lake. When he brought her back to the tribe they rejected her, so she placed a curse on the lake."

She takes a sip of her champagne. "Mmm…This is good."

"Where did you learn all this?" asked Smyth.

"Research, luv," Bess replied. "Wovoka told me."

"And just who is this Wovoka?" Smyth asked.

"Local tribal elder."

"Spirits and elders, huh," Smyth scoffed.

"And restless souls that slit fishermen's throats?" Bess countered, her voice firm. "Wovoka holds the key to understanding this place, its history, and its secrets. We can't dismiss his wisdom just because it doesn't fit your textbook definition of evidence."

She paused a beat. "There's something else. Wovoka mentioned Confederate gold hidden in the lake guarded by restless spirits."

"Must you keep mentioning spirits?" Abbott said nervously.

Smyth scoffed. "Gold and water spirits? Sounds like something out of a dime novel."

Bess's smile remained undeterred. "Maybe. But Wovoka, the local tribal elder, seems to think there's some truth to it. He claims to know where the spirits reside."

"And you think this Wovoka can help us find a killer?" Smyth asked, a flicker of interest sparkled in his eyes.

Bess leaned back, a triumphant smirk spread across her face. "That's exactly what I think."

"So, miss investigative reporter, where would you start?" asked Smyth.

"I think a visit with Wovoka for a start," she replied.

"And where would he be? On the reservation?"

"Yes. I already arranged a meeting with him."

"You're definitely more than efficient, young lady," Abbott remarked.

Smyth held himself against making a remark.

CHAPTER TWO

After checking the bags in their room, Bess led Smyth and Abbott to a dusty corral on the outskirts of Reno. Three sturdy horses awaited them, snorting impatiently.

"No stagecoach to the reservation, boys," Bess announced. "We're going old school."

Smyth eyed the horses with a practiced hand, selecting a chestnut gelding. Abbott, ever the city slicker, fumbled before mounting his own steed.

"How far to this reservation?" Abbott inquired, nervously adjusting his hat.

"Not far," Bess replied, already mounted on a sleek black mare. "Just a short ride around the perimeter of the lake."

An hour later, the stark beauty of the Paiute reservation unfolded before them. Patchwork of teepees, woven from branches and grass, dotted the rocky landscape.

Bess steered them towards a particularly large teepee with a feathered crown adorning its peak.

"Wait here," she instructed, dismounting her horse.

She approached the entrance, her voice barely a whisper as she spoke. "Wovoka. We are here."

A few moments later, a tall, lanky, Native-American man dressed in jeans, cowboy boots and a blue and white checkered shirt, exited the wickiup. The only concession to his Native-American dress was an elaborate feathered crown.

He eyed Smyth and Abbott with dark brown eyes sunken in a sun-drenched face.

Bess stepped in. "Wovoka. These are the men I told you about. They would like to talk to you."

Smyth and Abbott nodded politely, then Smyth asked, "Bess here told us you know a lot about the lake. We would appreciate if you could fill us in on what you know."

"They are looking for a murderer and they believe he is at the lake." Bess said. "And responsible for the deaths there."

There was a long pause as the three waited in anticipation of Wovoka's response. When it came, it wasn't very helpful.

"No human kills. Spirits kill."

"Spirits, huh?" Smyth replied. He looked at Bess. "I think we're done here," and turned to leave.

"Wait!" she said. Then turned to Wovoka. "You told me you knew where these spirits reside in the lake. Right?"

Wovoka nodded.

She nudged Smyth's arm. "Who or what is killing people doesn't matter. Let's have Wovoka show us. It might be what we are looking for." She turned to Wovoka. "Please, tell us what you know."

Wovoka nodded. "There are whispers of gold here. Guarded by restless spirits."

At the word 'spirits', Abbott shuffled his feet nervously.

Smyth gave him a disapproving glance. "Tell us more. Where do these 'spirits' reside."

"Lake has hidden coves and mythical underwater shelves and caves that can't be seen from surface," he began. "Much danger in the lake. The wind can be harsh. Speed and direction can change suddenly and dramatically. Because of this and the underwater structures, the currents in the lake can be unpredictable and dangerous."

"Can you show us these caves and shelves?" asked Smyth.

"Show, yes. Go, no," he replied.

"What does that mean?" asked Abbott.

The Paiute tribal leader replied, "Can point you to the lake. Then listen for the wails of the water babies." With that, he disappeared back into his wikiup.

"So, just take a row on the lake," stated Abbott, "and wait for these water babies to point out the place?"

Bess voiced the inevitable. "So, when Smyth?" "Bess. You and Abbott get us a boat. We leave tonight."

CHAPTER THREE

That evening, Bess secured a small fishing boat from a reluctant fisherman, his weathered face etched with worry. "You folks sure about this? The lake can be a fickle beast at night, especially under a full moon."

"We know the risks," Bess assured him, flashing a disarming smile that managed to ease some of the man's concern.

As the sun began its descent, casting long shadows across the desert landscape, they loaded their meager supplies into the boat and tied up their horses to a weathered tree stump.

"The boat is kind a small for three people," complained Abbott, "and it smells like rancid fish."

"This all I could find," Bess replied. "We just have to move the fishing nets and gear under our feet." Ever the planner, she said. "Alright, Smyth, you're at the helm. You know how to handle a boat, right?"

Smyth, his jaw clenched tight, gave a curt nod.

Abbott, his face pale, swallowed hard. As an afterthought, he gulped, "Glad we brought our side arms."

Bess chuckled, a dry humor lacing her voice. "Against spirits, Mr. Abbott? I don't think a six-shooter will do much good." She fingered the small knife attached to her leather belt.

Abbott's face went pale.

Nightfall descended swiftly, engulfing the world in an inky blackness. The full moon, a giant pearl in the velvet sky, cast an eerie glow on the water, creating a shimmering path that stretched out before them.

Smyth dipped the oars into the water, propelling the boat forward. The silence was broken only by the rhythmic laps of the water against the hull and the occasional creak of the boat timbers.

As they ventured deeper into the lake, a strange chill settled around them. The air seemed to crackle with an unseen energy, sending shivers down their spines.

Suddenly, a sound pierced the silence – a mournful wail that echoed across the water. It was a sound unlike anything they had ever heard, filled with a chilling despair that sent shivers down their spines.

Abbott jumped, his face contorted in fear. "Did you hear that?" he whispered, his voice barely a croak.

Bess, her eyes gleaming with an uncharacteristic nervousness, nodded slowly. "That's the sound Wovoka spoke of. The wail of the water babies. That way," she pointed.

Smyth steered the boat towards the source of the sound. Despite his skepticism, the raw, primal fear emanating from the wail was undeniable.

As they navigated deeper into the heart of the lake, the wails grew more frequently, their mournful cries weaving a haunting melody across the water. The moon's reflection on the surface shimmered and distorted, creating an unsettling mirage that blurred the line between reality and illusion.

Then, in the distance, a faint glow flickered on the water's edge. It pulsed rhythmically, beckoning them forward.

Bess leaned forward, her eyes wide with a mix of fear and curiosity. "Do you see that, Smyth? The light."

Smyth, steeling himself against the wails, steered the boat towards the enigmatic glow.

As they drew closer, the light resolved itself – a half-submerged cave entrance, its mouth glowing with an otherworldly luminescence.

Smyth guided the small boat to the cave as the air around it grew thick and heavy. With his hand hovering over the oars, he looked at Bess and Abbott.

"Are we sure about this?" Abbott asked, his voice barely a whisper.

Bess, her own fear evident, forced a smile. "We came this far, haven't we? The secrets of the lake might lie within."

With a deep breath, Smyth dipped the oars back into the water, propelling the boat towards the glowing mouth of the cave. The water churned around them, and the wails of the water babies reached a fever pitch as they entered the heart of the unknown.

The cold, damp air of the cave washed over them as they were about to dock with the cave's threshold.

Suddenly, the eerie luminescence emanating from the cave entrance faded, leaving them in near-total darkness. Only the rhythmic creak of the boat and the sound of dripping water broke the oppressive silence.

Bess fumbled in her bag, pulling out a small oil lamp. With a shaky hand, she struck a flint and wick, bathing the immediate area in a warm, flickering light. The meager illumination revealed jagged rock walls and a passage that sloped steeply downwards.

"Looks inviting, doesn't it?" Abbott quipped, his voice laced with nervous humor.

Bess ignored him, her gaze fixed on the passage ahead. "We need to be careful," she warned. "This place could be unstable."

Smyth was about to secure the boat to a rocky outcrop with the mooring rope when, suddenly, strong gusts of wind tore across the lake, whipping the water into a frenzy.

The boat lurched, rocking precariously.

"Hold on!" Smyth barked, his voice taut with alarm.

As if summoned by the wind, a swirling vortex of mist materialized off the starboard side. It roiled and churned, obscuring the water with an eerie white fog.

Panic choked Bess's throat, her mind conjuring images of vengeful spirits rising from the depths.

"What is that?" she gasped, her voice barely a whisper.

Smyth didn't answer. He wrestled with the tiller, fighting to control the boat as it was drawn towards the swirling vortex.

The mist grew thicker, swallowing them whole in its icy embrace. The air turned frigid, clinging to their skin like a shroud. Then, with a bone-jarring jolt, the boat hit something unseen, sending them sprawling from the craft as it capsized.

Bess sputtered, clinging to the overturned boat, the taste of lake water flooding her mouth. When the first wave of disorientation passed, she saw Smyth, half-submerged in the water, struggling to reach something beneath the overturned boat.

"Bess!" Abbott screamed, hanging onto the bow of the overturned boat. "There. Help Smyth!"

Without hesitation, Bess released her grip in the skiff and plunged in, diving into the murky depths. The lake water was ice-cold, stealing the breath from her lungs. She kicked and clawed, fighting the disorienting darkness, until she saw him – Smyth, entangled in a thick fishing net that fell off the fishing boat, the fabric taut against his chest.

Bess knew the danger of entangled nets. One wrong move, one panicked twist, and they could both be trapped for eternity. Taking a deep breath, she used her knife to carefully slice through the mesh, strand by strand. Her fingertips burned with the cold, but she pushed on, fueled by a fierce determination.

Finally, the net gave way. Smyth, gasping for air, surfaced beside her.

They clung to each other, hearts pounding in unison, their bodies battered by the unforgiving lake.

"Thank you," he said. "Thank you."

They swam over to the overturned boat and were successful in righting it up.

"Let's start bailing."

As the wind died down and the mist dissipated, the moonlight cast the lake in a strange luminescence. Looking around, they realized they were adrift, far from where they started.

The hidden cove seemed like a distant dream, lost in the swirling fog.

CHAPTER FOUR

Wovoka, a wiry silhouette against the moonlit lake, scanned the still water. The recent storm had whipped it into a frenzy, but now it lay placid, lapping innocently at the rocky shore. He spun on his heel and stalked back to his wikiup, the slap of his moccasins echoing on the dry earth.

Inside, bathed in the flickering light of a dying fire, hunched an old woman. Her frail frame, hanging on her by a threadbare blanket, seemed barely strong enough to hold the worn leather moccasins on her tiny feet. Before her lay a meager dinner, untouched.

From the shadows, a voice rasped, "They're not dead."

Wovoka whipped around, eyes flashing. A burly man emerged from the darkness, his face obscured by the brim of a wide hat. He was dressed in ill-fitting gray clothes, a jarring contrast to the earthy tones of the wikiup. "We pay good money to keep the lake's secrets alive, and prying eyes dead."

"The job's done," Wovoka snarled, his voice taut. "They went in, just like you asked. But the lake..." He gestured to the water outside, his voice heavy with something akin to dread.

"Done isn't good enough!" The stranger spat, advancing on Wovoka with menacing strides. "If they show their faces again, you silence them. Understand?" He reached the entrance of the wikiup, his silhouette framed by the moonlight. "If they come back — kill them." With a final, chilling glare, he melted back into the night.

The silence that followed was shattered by a ragged sob. Pamahas, tears glistening on her wrinkled cheeks, looked up at Wovoka, her voice trembling. "Those men... they took Tau-gu. My husband!"

"He shouldn't have been on the lake," Wovoka said, his voice hardening. "I warned him." He took a menacing step towards her. "And I warn you now, old woman. Not a word of this to anyone. Not a whisper."

But the dam had broken. Pamahas, fueled by grief and a sudden surge of defiance, rose to her full height, her bony frame surprisingly strong. "This madness has to stop!" she shrieked, her voice cracking with raw emotion.

Before she could speak another word, Wovoka lunged. A sickening slap echoed in the confined space of the wikiup as his hand connected with her face. The old woman crumpled, a broken doll, food scattering across the dirt floor.

Wovoka loomed over her, his voice a low growl. "You'll keep your silence," he threatened, "or you'll join your husband."

Pamahas slowly pulled herself up, her face a mask of pain and defiance. With a resolute limp, she hobbled towards the exit, her eyes promising retribution, a silent vow for justice.

25

CHAPTER FIVE

Smyth, Abbott, and Bess returned to their suite at the Riverside Hotel, a damp, shivering mess. The stench of horse sweat and lake water clung to them like a second skin. After a hasty scrub and a change of clothes, they huddled back in the common area, the fireplace offering scant comfort against the chill that had seeped into their bones.

Moonlight speared through the window. Abbott, ever the worrier, broke the tense silence. "So, what's the bright idea now? Please tell me it doesn't involve that infernal lake again."

Smyth's voice was a low growl. "What choice do we have? We need to get into that damned cave, one way or another."

Abbott's hands twisted together like a knot of anxiety. "I was afraid of that."

Bess, ever the pragmatist, began, "I'll secure another boat first thing in the morning—"

A curt rap on the door cut her off. Bess exchanged wary glances with the others before cautiously pulling open the door.

A frail figure, cloaked in a threadbare blanket, stood in the doorway. "May I be of assistance?" Bess inquired, her voice laced with suspicion.

The old woman, a Paiute by the weathered look of her, pushed past Bess with surprising strength, her voice a mere rasp. "Talk. Now. Not much time."

Smyth boomed from across the room, "Who is it?"

Pamahas turned towards the sound, her gaze locking onto Smyth. "We need to speak. Quickly. You seek the cave in the lake, don't you?" Her voice dropped to a conspiratorial whisper as she darted a glance towards the moonlit window.

Smyth's eyes narrowed. "Indeed, we do. But how did you know?"

Fear flickered in the woman's eyes. "Wovoka. He tried to kill you. Lied to you. I offer truth."

Bess leaned forward, her curiosity piqued. "What kind of truth?"

The woman's voice dropped. "My husband, Tau-gu, sought the whispers of gold in the lake. He knew a path... a way to the cave that bypassed that cursed water." Her voice cracked, and she lowered her head. "He died for it. Found lifeless in his boat."

Bess ushered the woman towards a chair. "Please, sit. Tell us more. This path, you say?"

Pamahas' voice gained a tremor of excitement. "Tau-gu spoke of a way to cross on foot. When the moon hangs high, and the water is at its lowest."

Smyth straightened, a jolt of electricity coursing through him. "On foot? You can't be serious."

"Can you show us?" Bess pleaded.

Pamahas shook her head sadly. "I know only what Tau-gu shared. On the far side of the lake, a trail lies hidden amongst the scrub, leading straight to the caves."

"Please," Bess begged. "At least show us from the lake."

The old woman nodded.

But uncertainty flickered across Abbott's face. "Do we still need a boat? You mentioned your husband..."

"No," the woman rasped. "He used the boat to retrieve the gold. The caves can be reached by land."

Bess locked eyes with Smyth, a spark of determination igniting in her gaze. "It's a gamble, but one worth taking."

Smyth, a grim smile playing on his lips, declared, "Then we leave tonight."

CHAPTER SIX

The full moon hung low on the horizon, casting long, skeletal shadows across the dusty landscape. Smyth, Bess, and Abbott huddled behind a gnarled, wind-battered bush, their breaths misting in the pre-dawn chill.

Pamahas stood a few paces ahead, her silhouette blending seamlessly with the scrub. Her eyes, however, gleamed with an unnatural sharpness in the moonlight.

"There," she rasped, her voice barely a whisper. "See the faint trail, just beyond the rocks?"

Smyth squinted, following her bony finger. A barely discernible path snaked through the sparse vegetation, leading towards the distant silhouette of the lake. It looked more like a game trail for desert rodents than a path meant for humans.

"Are you sure this is it," Abbott asked, his voice barely above a squeak.

The old woman shot him a withering look. "Tau-gu never lied. That path leads to a hidden entrance on the western side of the cave. But remember," she added, her voice dropping to an even lower register, "the water can be most treacherous. Stay close to the rocks. One wrong step..." she trailed off, letting the unspoken threat hang heavy in the air.

A shiver ran down Bess's spine. The thought of navigating a treacherous path with a dark, churning water beside them wasn't exactly comforting.

Smyth shouldered his backpack and adjusted his gear. "Alright, let's move. We need to reach the cave before sunrise. And check your sidearms."

The journey was arduous.

The path was barely a path at all, more of a suggestion in the rocky terrain. Loose rock crunched under their boots, sending cascades of pebbles skittering down the slope. The silence was broken only by the rasp of their breath and the eerie cry of a nocturnal bird.

As they neared the lake, the air grew thick with the damp smell of fresh water and decaying vegetation. The moon, now a pale smudge in the lightening sky, cast an ethereal glow on the water, making it appear deceptively calm. However, Smyth knew better. He could almost feel the unseen currents tugging at the rocky shoreline.

They reached a narrow, rocky ledge that jutted out into the lake. Below them, the water churned, a menacing black abyss.

"That is it," said Smyth, pointing towards a dark opening nestled amongst the craggy rocks opposite them. "The entrance to the cave."

Bess swallowed hard. The sheer audacity of attempting to cross such a treacherous expanse of water sent a wave of dizziness washing over her.

Smyth, however, seemed unfazed. He unfurled a length of rope he had brought with him, securing one end to a sturdy rock on their side.

"Alright, listen up," he said, his voice firm. "We'll cross one at a time. I'll go first, then Abbott, then Bess. Hold onto the rope for dear life. No heroics, understand?"

A tense silence followed his command. Finally, Abbott, his face pale with fear, nodded mutely.

Smyth took a deep breath, the rope feeling rough and reassuring in his hands. He stepped onto the ledge, the wind whipping at his face, the water roaring a constant challenge below. With a silent prayer, he lowered himself down the rocky face, the churning water seemingly reaching out to claim him.

The first few steps were the worst. The rope offered scant comfort. The growing wind threatened to yank him into the unforgiving water. But Smyth persevered. His determination hardened with each precarious step.

Finally, after what seemed like an eternity, he reached the other side, scrambling onto the rocky shore. Relief washed over him.

He secured the rope to a nearby outcrop, his gaze fixed on the two figures silhouetted against the lightening sky. Moments later, Abbott appeared, his face etched with fear and determination. His progress was slower, more cautious, but eventually, he too made it safely across.

Only Bess remained. Her fear was palpable, her grip on the rope white-knuckled. As she descended, the rope swayed precariously in the wind. Suddenly, a tremor ran through the line, a sickening snap echoing across the water.

Smyth's heart lurched. The rope. It had snapped. He watched in horror as Bess, suspended mid-air, let out a cry. Her grip on the remaining frayed end faltered.

Bess screamed, her voice a thin thread lost in the howling wind. Smyth scrambled towards the edge, adrenaline surging through his veins. He could barely make out Bess's flailing form.

Without a moment's hesitation, Smyth lunged. His fingers brushed the rocky ledge, but it was just out of reach. With a desperate grunt, he strained against the wind, pushing himself closer. But Bess slipped through his grasp.

Smyth dared not look down. His stomach churned with a sickening dread.

CHAPTER SEVEN

The world tilted when a sickening lurch yanked Bess from her freefall. A vice clamped around her wrist, pulling her into and onto a ledge. As she spun around, a figure loomed out of the shadows, clad in the unmistakable gray of a Confederate uniform. Wovoka's warnings about restless spirits echoed in her mind, chilling her blood. But as her vision cleared, the apparition solidified into a young man, broad-shouldered and handsome in a dangerous way.

"Quite a tumble, miss," he drawled, a hint of amusement dancing in his dark eyes. "Lucky I was here to catch you." He looked past and her over her head. "What brings you out here alone on a night like this? Anyone with you?"

Dazed, Bess shook her head. "Uh…No." Her lie was weak and she knew he didn't believe her.

His gaze flicked back to her. "Not the smartest time for a solo mountain climb, is it?"

The soldier wasn't asking. It was an order.

A cold knot of dread formed in Bess's stomach. Her fingers instinctively searched for the familiar weight of her pistol at her hip - only to find emptiness. She was at his mercy.

"You'd best come with me," he said, the amusement gone, replaced by a steely glint.

Bess had no choice. She was a rabbit caught in the headlights of a rebel soldier's dark intentions.

CHAPTER EIGHT

"Bess," Abbott pressed, his voice edged with desperation. "Where is she? Do you think she's alive?"

"I don't know," he said, his voice cold as ice. "But perhaps..." then chased the thought from his mind. "We're here at the cave. Let's move forward. We have to see this through".

The cave mouth yawned before them, a dark, gaping maw. They cautiously approached the cave and hesitated only a moment as the cave entrance swallowed them whole. A sliver of dawning light was the only illumination in the cave. But that too soon disappeared as they moved deeper into the cavern.

Smyth fumbled for the lantern in his backpack and lit it. Its beam cut through the inky void like a lifeline. Strange shadows danced and writhed on the cavern walls, taking on grotesque shapes in the flickering light. The air was thick with the scent of damp earth and decay.

A sudden glimmer of light caught Smyth's eye, a distant beacon in the darkness. They pressed on as the passage widened into a cavernous chamber, its ceiling lost in impenetrable blackness.

Then a voice, cold and menacing, echoed behind them. The two men turned to see, bathed in the light of several oil lamps. A ring of Confederate soldiers emerged from the shadows. Their faces lit by the warm glow of oil lamps. Pistols glinted in the dim light, aimed squarely at the two intruders.

A burly sergeant, his face a mask of hatred, barked an order, "Search 'em, boys. Tie 'em up. Take 'em to headquarters."

CHAPTER NINE

"Now, doesn't this look familiar?" Burnside sneered, his voice a cold whip crack in the cavernous space. Three Confederate goons flanked him, their faces etched with the same chilling malice.

"Burnside," Abbott hissed, his voice barely audible.

Smyth, never one to mince words, said with a sneer, "The rat's back in a hole, is it?"

Burnside ignored the taunt.

"So, what's your game here," Smyth added, "besides slitting throats of lake visitors?"

"The lake's reputation," Burnside stated, "as told by the local tribe, gives me cover for your, let us say, interference with my plans in Prescott. The curse of the Water Babies, as the Paiute say, keeps prying visitors as yourselves way from our plans."

Abbott's jaw clenched. "You still dream of your damn Confederacy, don't you?"

Burnside's lips curled into a sinister smile. "Always have, always will."

Smyth's voice was sharp. "But the explosion, the fire in the town tunnels - that set you back. Destroyed your organization and wiped out your cash."

Burnside's smile widened, revealing a flash of predatory teeth. "Set back? Perhaps. These men here are all I have left of my organization. But only temporarily." His gaze flickered to Smyth. "By the way, did you find any gold down there in the Prescott tunnels?"

Smyth shook his head.

"Good," Burnside said, his voice laced with satisfaction. "The gold wasn't there. It was up here, hidden in this labyrinth. The curse was just a cherry on top."

Abbott's eyes narrowed. "But the rumors about Confederate gold here..."

"Exactly. And those who came looking for it...well, they became part of the legend." Burnside laughed, the sound echoing through the cavern.

A commotion erupted at the cavern's entrance. Two figures emerged, one struggling against the other's grip.

"Your boys found a feisty little redhead outside," Wovoka sneered, a glint of triumph in his eyes.

"Bess!" Abbott exclaimed, relief and hope washing over him.

Smyth's voice was a hoarse whisper. "You're, okay?"

Bess was about to speak when Burnside cut her off.

"Enough with the reunion. You two," pointing at the two men, "are going to meet the real curse of this place." He gestured towards Wovoka. "Show them the way."

"What about the woman?" Smyth demanded.

"Not to worry," Wovoka sneered, "We have special plans for her. We'll make a special example of her."

Smyth was about to respond, when he felt the cold hard steel jab him in the back. The three Confederates then herded Smyth and Abbott at gunpoint through a twisting, damp passage. Time seemed to stretch into eternity as they stumbled through the darkness. Finally, Wovoka barked a command to stop.

Before them lay a yawning chasm, the sound of rushing water echoing from its depths. "Perfect timing," one of the Confederates said, his voice filled with grim satisfaction. "The tide is going out."

Wovoka's eyes gleamed with a cruel light. "And you're going out with it."

With brutal efficiency, the Confederates shoved their captives into the abyss.

CHAPTER TEN

It was all Smyth and Abbott could do to keep their heads above the swirling water. Abbott, his face contorted in agony, was struggling the most.

"Kick, damn it, Charles!" Smyth bellowed.

Abbott's face was a mask of white-knuckled terror. "I can't!" he gasped. His damaged leg, a useless, burning weight, dragging him under.

Smyth, fighting the building current, swam over to Abbott and hauled him onto his chest. "Hold on, damn it!" he shouted. "Don't move."

Swimming backwards carrying Abbott on his chest, he saw a glimmer of hope – a battered, ghostly shape emerging from the fog.

A boat. A lifeline. A miracle.

"Help!" he screamed, his voice a desperate plea carried away on the wind. "Anyone! Help. Please!"

No answer.

He strained against the waves, pushing him and Abbott towards the boat. When he grabbed hold of the side of the boat, he realized it was empty. He pushed Abbott into the boat and with a final, desperate surge, Smyth hauled himself over the boat's slippery side.

As they collapsed, gasping for air, Abbott's voice was weak. "What's an abandoned boat doing out here?" Abbott asked.

"Let's not look a gift horse in the mouth. We have to find Bess," his voice filled with grim determination.

Smyth huffed and puffed, raising the sail of the small fishing boat and pointed the craft towards the waves crashing against the rocks of the cave. He powered the small boat through the swirling water and docked it at the mouth of the cavern entrance.

"You stay here with the boat," he told Abbott.

"No. I'm coming with you."

"But your leg. Shouldn't you...?"

Abbott cut him off. "I'm coming. For Bess's sake."

As they entered the cavern, the dim glow of a campfire came into view. Two Confederate sentries sat by the fire, their silhouettes stark against the darkness.

"Sentries," Abbott whispered. "We have no weapons." his voice trembling slightly.

"They do," Smyth replied.

"Then I'll distract them," Abbott said, his voice low. "You take them from behind me."

Smyth picked up a rock, the weight solid in his hand. With a silent nod, he slipped into the shadows behind Abbott as he hobbled towards the Confederates, his injured leg a clear disadvantage.

"What the...? You're supposed to be dead!" one of the soldiers exclaimed seeing Abbott.

"Boo!" Smyth shouted from behind and threw the rock at one of the Confederates, hitting him square in the face.

The man screamed in pain, blood flowing into his eyes.

The second Confederate lunged for his rifle, but Abbott, with a desperate surge of adrenaline, tackled him, sending them both crashing into the campfire.

In the chaos, Smyth disarmed the injured soldier while Abbott struggled free from the flames while he disarmed his charge.

"Good job, Charles. Bloody good job." He patted Abbott on his smoldering back. "You better stay back with the boat and nurse your leg. I'll get Bess."

"How will you find her?'

"I find Burnside and I find her." Smyth's voice was low and trailed off as he squinted into the gloom.

CHAPTER ELEVEN

The cavern was a tomb of cold, damp darkness. Smyth's breath fogged the air as he traveled the cavern tunnels using a dimming oil lamp. At a passageway between two tunnels, he chose the one on the left. "I think this looks familiar," he said to himself.

He didn't venture far when a sharp command cut through the silence behind him. "That's far enough!"

He whirled, gun drawn, into the sharp glare of an oil lamp. Wovoka, a menacing figure, stood with a Confederate soldier at his side, both weapons leveled.

"You should be dead!" Wovoka growled.

Smyth's lips curved in a wry smile. "Seems to be a popular opinion."

"Enough of your wit," Wovoka pointed his horse pistol at Smyth's head. "No fancy executions this time." He nodded to the Confederate at his side, who imitated Wovoka and cocked his pistol at Abbott. "This will be easy. Now down on your knees."

Smyth obeyed, kneeling defiant, a question burning his lips, "The girl? Is she alive?"

"She's being attended to by the Colonel," the soldier smirked.

"She'll join you shortly," Wovoka grinned.

A raspy voice boomed from behind, "Not before you!"

Wovoka turned to see Pamahas pointing a rifle at him. He turned to confront her, but she fired her long gun, putting a well-placed shot into his chest. He fell at Smyth's feet.

"That's for Tau-gu!" she spit.

The Confederate, now distracted, gave Smyth the chance he needed. He half stood and threw himself at the soldier, landing hard against the wall of the cavern. His pistol flying across the ground. The Confederate recovered quickly, drew his knife and went after Smyth.

But Smyth grabbed the pistol at his feet and shot the soldier before he could reach him.

He stood up and turned to Pamahas. "It was *your* abandoned boat!"

She nodded. "I had a score to settle with Wovoka."

"So, do I. With that Colonel," Smyth replied. "He has Bess."

"I can help with that," the Paiute countered." I know where he is."

"Good," Smyth replied. "Lead the way."

CHAPTER TWELVE

Equipped with Wovoka's and Pamahas' lantern, Smyth followed the Paiute woman through the winding tunnels of the cavern until they reached Burnside's makeshift headquarters.

"Empty," she sighed, clutching her long gun. "He must have heard the gunshots echoing through the cave."

Smyth thought for moment. "If you were him, sitting on a pile of gold, his cover blown, what would you do?"

"Why, get it off the lake!" the old woman replied with a grin.

Then a troubled thought hit Smyth. "Either he humped it over the land route we took or...my God! Abbott!"

Smyth hurried back to the cavern entrance with Pamahas in tow. When they arrived, they saw Abbott, under the steady pistol of Burnside, dragging bags of gold to the fishing boat tied up at the cave entrance.

Next to the skiff was Bes, tied to a nearby rock, a gag in her mouth.

Both Smyth and the old woman stepped out of the tunnel and drew their sidearms.

Abbott looked up at Smyth and wearily said, "Thank God you're here!" He turned his rancor on Burnside. "Wanker!"

Burnside just grinned. "I assumed Mr. Abbott's comment is not a compliment."

"Just drop your gun," Smyth replied. "What kind of a man are you?" sneered Smyth, leveling his pistol at Burnside. "Using a crippled man to be your slave. Just like a Confederate slave owner."

Smyth pointed at Bess. "And tying up a helpless woman."

Abbott untied Bess and removed her gag.

As soon as Bess was free and her gag removed, she walked over to Burnside and punched him square in the face. Then followed a tirade of Scottish insults aimed at Burnside that even Smyth had never heard.

"Your game is over, Burnside," Smyth snarled.

"So, it seems," Burnside replied. "But Wovoka will be here soon with my men. Then we'll see."

"He's not coming," Pamahas smiled. "He dead. I shot him."

"He was right about you." Burnside growled. "You were a liability and should have been shot." He pulled his hand inside the sleeve of his blouse and withdrew a small derringer. And leveled it at the old woman.

Bess, seeing this, jumped at Burnside.

He fired and hit Bess who stumbled backwards and collapsed at Smyth's feet.

Everyone rushed to Bess giving Burnside a chance to flee through the cave, dragging bags of gold with him.

Smyth cradled Bess's head in his lap, stunned at the turn of events.

"Get that bastard, Smyth" Abbott yelled.

Smyth stood up and said to Pamahas, "Take care of her. Please." Then, with grim determination, he followed after Burnside.

* * * * *

Burnside halted abruptly, his breath coming in ragged gasps. With a frantic efficiency, he lashed the remaining bags of gold to his body. Looking back behind him, he moved as fast as he could down the slippery tunnels of the cave.

Smyth emerged from the tunnel. The pit that he and Abbott were thrown into by Wovoka loomed at the end of the passage.

"That's far enough, you bastard," Smyth demanded.

Burnside turned with his back to the pit and the swirling lake below.

Smyth advanced towards Burnside, pointing his pistol. "You may have killed Bess. You're a dead man walking."

"So, the great British sleuth will kill in cold blood? That not very sporting of you chap - as they say in England."

Smyth continued to advance on Burnside. "Perhaps you're right. I'll settle for watching you hang for what you've done."

Burnside smiled knowing he has cheated death for now. He steps back to adjust his balance when the gravel and small rocks under his feet begins to give way.

Smyth watches Burnside, whose eyes are filled with terror.

"Don't let me fall!" he screams.

Smyth picks up one of the bags a gold that fell from Burnside. "On second thought, why don't you see your dream of a second Confederacy? You'll need these" as he throws the heavy bag of gold at Burnside.

It hits the Colonel in the chest and he, and the gold tied to him, go head over heels into the pit of swirling lake water below.

The impact was a sickening thud, followed by a series of bubbles as the gold-laden corpse disappeared beneath the surface.

CHAPTER THIRTEEN

"How are you feeling," asked Smyth.

"The doc said I'd be all right," Bess replied, adjusting her bedclothes in her hospital bed. "The bullet didn't hit any major organs. Should be up and around in a few days."

"That's good news," Abbott said.

He went on. "You know, Burnside had a good thing going," he mused. "Using that Water Babies curse to scare off gold hunters was pure genius." He paused, his brow furrowed. "But those wails we heard on the lake. They were real, weren't they?"

Bess's eyes held a strange intensity. "I think they were," she replied, her voice low.

Smyth couldn't resist a teasing grin. "Spirits again, Bess? You and your ghost stories."

She shot him a withering glare. "You underestimate me, Smyth. If I told you what I think..."

"Please, spare us," Smyth retorted, holding up his hands in mock surrender. "No more tales of your intrepid reporter days."

Their banter was interrupted by a nurse's aide who walked into the hospital room. "This came for you, Miss Bess." She handed her a telegram.

Bess thanked her and opened it. A wide grin spread across her face as she read.

"Gentlemen," she announced triumphantly, "This is what I was waiting for. The hunt is not over. We are off to New York."

THE CASE OF THE DEATHLY WATER BABIES OF PYRAMID LAKE

To Be Continued in The Finale of

Johnathan Smyth: Cowboy Sleuth

'The Case of the Murder Mansion'

Buck Brannan leaned against the worn pew of the small chapel, his gaze fixed on the stained-glass window depicting a lone rider against a setting sun. His face, etched with lines from years in the saddle and kissed a deep brown by the desert sun, held a hint of impatience. It also wore an old scar that ran down the left side of his face - half closing his eye to his jowls - a testament to a past encounter, adding a touch of menace to his features.

 "Tell me," he pressed. The question to Maggie Star, the young nurse's aide at the hospital, was less a request and more of a demand.

"Not here," Maggie replied, her voice low. She glanced around the empty chapel, her eyes darting towards the entrance. Buck's reputation wasn't exactly a secret. "There's a small cafe down the street. We can talk there."

A few minutes later, they were seated at a corner table, the soft hum of conversation providing a backdrop to their urgent discussion.

"Now," Buck said, leaning forward, "what did you find out? What was in that telegram?"

Maggie hesitated, her fingers tracing the rim of her coffee cup. "You were right about them. They're investigators chasing Jack the Ripper. The telegram was to Bess, a reporter with them. I couldn't hear the exact contents, but I overheard Bess exclaim that the lead pointed them to New York."

"New York?" Buck repeated, his brow furrowing. "That's it? Nothing else?"

"Yes. One other thing. They're going to look for a seaman there."

She paused, her eyes meeting his. "When do I get paid?"

Buck reached into his worn leather vest and pulled out a twenty-dollar gold piece. "Here." He tossed it onto the table. "And keep this to ourselves. This conversation never happened."

Maggie fingered the coin, a flicker of amusement crossing her face. "What conversation?"

Johnathan Smyth: Cowboy Sleuth

Series Titles

BOOK 1 'The Case of the Screaming Tunnel'

BOOK 2 'The Case of the Lost Ship In The Desert'

BOOK 3 'The Case of the Red Ghost Camel'

BOOK 4 'The Case of the Prescott Tunnels'

BOOK 5 'The Case of the Deathly Water Babies of Pyramid Lake

BOOK 6 'The Case of the Murder Mansion'